Dear Parent:

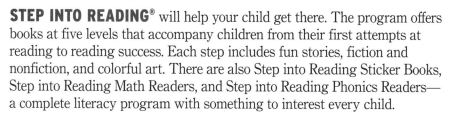

Congratulations! Your child is taking the first steps on an exciting journey. The destination? Independent reading!

STEP INTO READING® will help your child get there. The program offers books at five levels that accompany children from their first attempts at reading to reading success. Each step includes fun stories, fiction and nonfiction, and colorful art. There are also Step into Reading Sticker Books, Step into Reading Math Readers, and Step into Reading Phonics Readers— a complete literacy program with something to interest every child.

Learning to Read, Step by Step!

Ready to Read   Preschool–Kindergarten
• big type and easy words • rhyme and rhythm • picture clues
For children who know the alphabet and are eager to begin reading.

Reading with Help   Preschool–Grade 1
• basic vocabulary • short sentences • simple stories
For children who recognize familiar words and sound out new words with help.

Reading on Your Own   Grades 1–3
• engaging characters • easy-to-follow plots • popular topics
For children who are ready to read on their own.

Reading Paragraphs   Grades 2–3
• challenging vocabulary • short paragraphs • exciting stories
For newly independent readers who read simple sentences with confidence.

Ready for Chapters   Grades 2–4
• chapters • longer paragraphs • full-color art
For children who want to take the plunge into chapter books but still like colorful pictures.

STEP INTO READING® is designed to give every child a successful reading experience. The grade levels are only guides. Children can progress through the steps at their own speed, developing confidence in their reading no matter what their grade.

f reading starts with a single step!

For Raymond's aunts:
Katherine, Lucy, Stephanie, Uma, and Lori
—V.M.N.

For Cheryl—D.A.

Text copyright © 2002 by Vaunda Micheaux Nelson.
Illustrations copyright © 2002 by Derek Anderson.
All rights reserved under International and Pan-American Copyright Conventions.
Published in the United States by Random House Children's Books, a division of Random House,
Inc., New York, and simultaneously in Canada by Random House of Canada Limited, Toronto.

www.stepintoreading.com

Educators and librarians, for a variety of teaching tools,
visit us at www.randomhouse.com/teachers

Library of Congress Cataloging-in-Publication Data
Nelson, Vaunda Micheaux.
Ready? Set. Raymond! / by Vaunda Micheaux Nelson ;
illustrated by Derek Anderson.
p. cm. — (Step into reading. A step 2 book)
SUMMARY: Three stories in which a little boy does everything fast, from brushing his teeth
to making friends to running races.
ISBN 0-375-81363-2 (trade) — ISBN 0-375-91363-7 (lib. bdg.)
[1. Speed—Fiction.] I. Anderson, Derek, ill. II. Title. III. Series: Step into reading. Step 2 book.
PZ7.N43773 Re 2002 [E]—dc21 2002013347

Printed in the United States of America 11 10 9 8 7 6 5 4 3

STEP INTO READING, RANDOM HOUSE, and the Random House colophon are registered trademarks
of Random House, Inc.

Ready? Set. Raymond!

by Vaunda Micheaux Nelson

illustrated by Derek Anderson

Random House 🏠 New York

Slow Down, Raymond

Raymond does

things fast.

He brushes his teeth fast.

He eats breakfast fast.

"Slow down, Raymond.
Chew your food,"
Mama says.

Raymond slows down—
but not for long!

Raymond
dresses fast.

He kisses
Mama fast.

He runs
to school
fast.

"Slow down, Raymond.
Look both ways,"
the policeman says.

Raymond slows down—
but not for long!

He reads fast.

He counts fast.

He draws
pictures fast.

"Slow down, Raymond. There's no rush," his teacher says.

Raymond slows down— but not for long!

He runs
home fast.

He eats
dinner fast.

He brushes his
teeth fast.

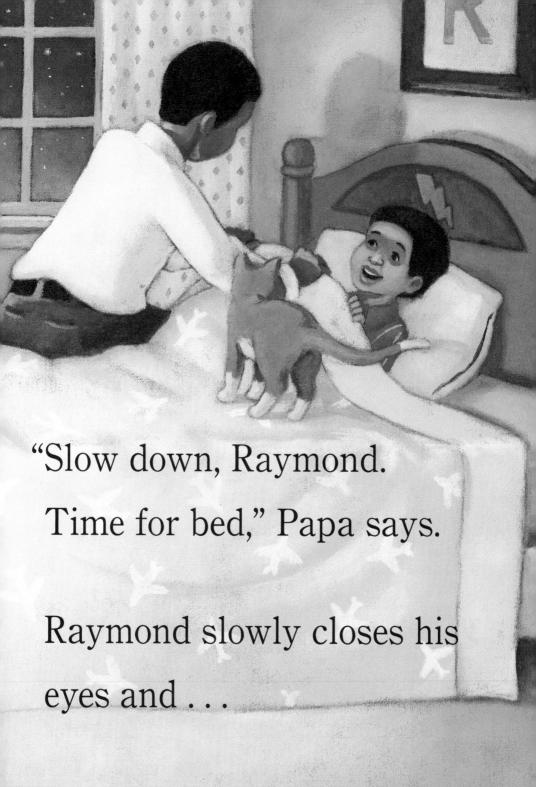

"Slow down, Raymond.
Time for bed," Papa says.

Raymond slowly closes his
eyes and . . .

... falls _fast_ asleep!

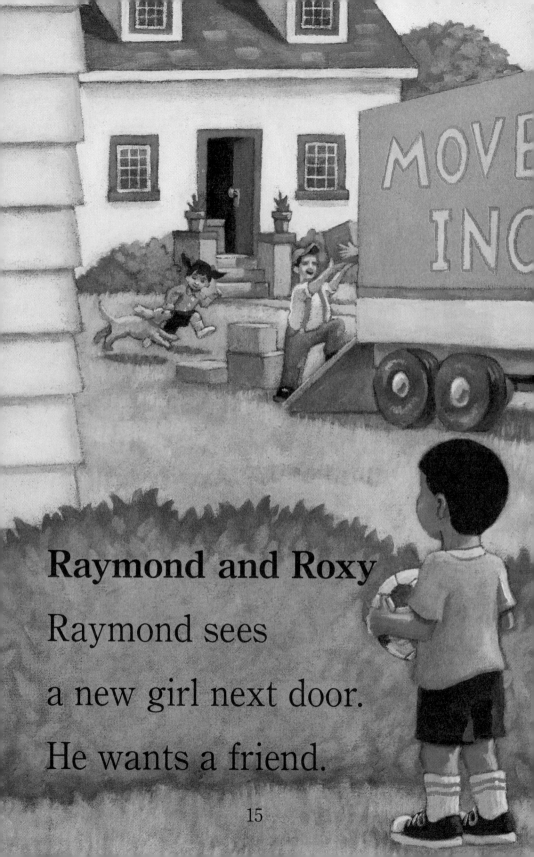

Raymond and Roxy

Raymond sees
a new girl next door.
He wants a friend.

"Making friends
takes time,"
Mama says.

But Raymond cannot wait.

He runs next door.

"I'm Raymond!" he says.

The girl runs inside.

Raymond <u>walks</u> home.

"Making friends
takes time,"
Papa says.

But Raymond cannot wait.

He runs to the cookie jar.

He runs next door.

Raymond gives the girl
a cookie.

She takes a bite.

She smiles with cookie
in her teeth.

"I'm Roxy," she says.

Raymond and Roxy

become <u>fast</u> friends.

New Sneakers

Raymond likes to run.
He is going to be
in a big race.

He runs in the house,

in the yard,

at the park.

Raymond runs so much

he wears his sneakers out!
Mama buys Raymond
brand-new sneakers
for the big race.
They are white,
like clean sheets.

Raymond wants
his sneakers
to stay clean.
So he walks slowly
in the house,

in the yard,

to the park.

The race is starting.

"Ready?"

Raymond looks

at the dusty track.

"Set."

Raymond looks at
his clean new sneakers.

"Go!"

"Run, Raymond, run!"

Roxy shouts.

Raymond runs.

His sneakers get dirty.

But he wins the race!